The Little U
An Inspirational Diary
for Young Ladies

L. M. Alcott (signature)

Louisa May Alcott
November 29, 1832 – March 6, 1888

American author and poet, best known for her beloved novel
Little Women. Published in 1868, *Little Women* is set in the
Alcott family home, Orchard House, in Concord,
Massachusetts, and is loosely based on Alcott's childhood
experiences with her three sisters.

"Human minds are more full of mysteries than any written book and more changeable than the cloud shapes in the air."

"Sometimes when we least expect it, a small cross proves a lovely crown, a seemingly unimportant event becomes a lifelong experience, or a stranger becomes a friend"

"It's not half so sensible to leave legacies when one dies as it is to use the money wisely while alive, and enjoy making one's fellow creatures happy with it."

"I don't pretend to be wise, but I am observing, and I see a great deal more than you'd imagine."

"Young people think they never can change, but they do in the most wonderful manner, and very few die of broken hearts."

"Preserve your memories, keep them well, what you forget you can never retell."

"Color makes no difference, the peeps are gray, the seals are black, and the crabs yellow, but we don't care, and are all friends."

"I almost wish I hadn't any conscience, it's so inconvenient. If I didn't care about doing the right and didn't feel uncomfortable when doing wrong, I should get on capitally."

"I do like men who come out frankly and own that they are not gods."

"By gentle words and silent acts of kindness, he had won her reverence and her trust, which now had deepened into woman's truest, purest love."

_____

_____

_____

_____

_____

_____

_____

_____

_____

_____

_____

_____

_____

_____

_____

_____

_____

_____

_____

_____

_____

_____

"Time erodes all such beauty, but what it cannot diminish is the wonderful workings of your mind: Your humor, your kindness, and your moral courage."

"Many men can be what the world calls great: very few men are what God calls good."

"There is very little real liberty in the world, even those who seem freest are often the most tightly bound. Law, custom, public opinion, fear or shame make slaves of us all..."

"His love and care never tire or change, can never be taken from you, but may become the source of lifelong peace, happiness and strength."

"Do the things you know, and you shall learn the truth you need to know."

"life and love are very precious when both are in full bloom."

"You have so many extraordinary gifts, how can you expect to lead an ordinary life?"

"If we are all alive ten years hence, let's meet, and see how many of us have got our wishes, or how much nearer we are then than now."

"We all have our own kind of life to pursue, our own kind of dream to be weaving, and we all have the power to make wishes come true, as long as we keep believing."

"Wouldn't it be fun if all the castles in the air which we make could come true and we could live in them?"

"Love is the only thing that we can carry with us when we go, and it makes the end so easy."

"You are like a chestnut burr, prickly outside, but silky-soft within, and a sweet kernel, if one can only get at it. Love will make you show your heart one day, and then the rough burr will fall off."

"A real gentleman is as polite to a little girl as to a woman."

"When you feel discontented, think over your blessings, and be grateful."

"The fun and fame do not last, while the memory of a real helper is kept green long after poetry is forgotten and music silent."

"I'd take it manfully, and be respected if I couldn't be loved"

"Don't cry so bitterly, but remember this day, and resolve with all your soul that you will never know another like it."

"Our actions are in our own hands, but the consequences of them are not. Remember that, my dear, and think twice before you do anything."

"Beautiful souls often get put into plain bodies, but they cannot be hidden, and have a power all their own, the greater for the unconsciousness or the humility which gives it grace."

"Nothing provokes speculation more than the sight of a woman enjoying herself."

"Writing away at her novel with all her heart and soul, for till that was finished she could find no peace."

"A happy soul in a healthy body makes the best sort of beauty for man or woman."

"It takes two flints to make a fire."

"Love will make you show your heart someday..."

"Take some books and read, that's an immense help, and books are always good company if you have the right sort."

"Stay is a charming word in a friend's vocabulary."

"I don't envy her much, in spite of her money, for after all rich people have about as many worries as poor ones, I think"

"I do think that families are the most beautiful things in all the world!"

_____

_____

_____

_____

_____

_____

_____

_____

_____

_____

_____

_____

_____

_____

_____

_____

_____

_____

_____

_____

"You don't need scores of suitors. You need only one… if he's the right one."

"A quick temper, sharp tongue, and restless spirit were always getting her into scrapes, and her life was a series of ups and downs, which were both comic and pathetic."

"Keep bobbing, and we'll come right by and by."

"Love is a flower that grows in any soil, works its sweet miracles undaunted by autumn frost or winter snow, blooming and fragrant all the year, blessing those who give who receive."

"The more you love and trust him, the nearer you will feel to him, and the less you will depend on human power and wisdom."

_____

_____

_____

_____

_____

_____

_____

_____

_____

_____

_____

_____

_____

_____

_____

_____

_____

_____

_____

_____

"Some people seemed to get all sunshine, and some all shadow..."

"The humblest tasks get beautified if loving hands do them."

"If you dear little girls would only learn what real beauty is, and not pinch and starve and bleach yourselves out so, you'd save an immense deal of time and money and pain."

"Go out more, keep cheerful as well as busy, for you are the sunshine-maker of the family, and if you get dismal there is no fair weather."

"Let us be elegant or die!"

"Learn to know and value the praise which is worth having, and to excite the admiration of excellent people by being modest as well as pretty"

"Well, if I can't be happy, I can be useful, perhaps."

"Every genuine act or word, no matter how trifling it seems, leaves a sweet and strengthening influence behind"

"Young things like you don't need any ornaments but those you wear tonight: youth, health, intelligence, and modesty."

"Help one another is part of the religion of our sisterhood."

"There is not much danger that real talent or goodness will be overlooked long..."

"It's wicked to throw away so many good gifts because you can't have the one you want."

"I'd rather see you poor men's wives, if you were happy, beloved, contented, than queens on thrones, without self-respect and peace."

"Be comforted, dear soul! There is always light behind the clouds."

"It takes people a long time to learn the difference between talent and genius, especially ambitious young men and women."

"Virtue, which means honour, honesty, courage, and all that makes character, is the red thread that marks a good man wherever he is."

"Believe this heartily, and go to God with all your little cares, and hopes, and sins, and sorrows, as freely and confidingly as you come to your mother."

"I will make a battering-ram of my head and make a way through this rough-and-tumble world."

"Now and then, in this workaday world, things do happen in the delightful storybook fashion, and what a comfort that is."

"Wild roses are fairest, and nature a better gardener than art."

"Far away there in the sunshine are my highest aspirations. I may not reach them, but I can look up and see their beauty, believe in them, and try to follow where they lead."

"I don't like favors, they oppress and make me fell
like a slave. I'd rather do everything for myself,
and be perfectly independent."

"Many wise and true sermons are preached us everyday by unconscious ministers in street, school, office, or home"

"He was a fine man, my dear, but what is better, he was a brave and an honest one, and I was proud to be his friend."

"Conceit spoils the finest genius."

"If I didn't care about doing right and didn't feel uncomfortable doing wrong, I should get on capitally."

"Keep good company, read good books, love good things and cultivate soul and body as faithfully as you can"

"Hope and keep busy, and whatever happens,
remember that you never can be fatherless."

"I dare say, short answers save trouble."

"Our burdens are here, our road is before us, and the longing for goodness and happiness is the guide that leads us through many troubles to the peace which is a true Celestial City."

"Girls are so queer you never know what they mean. They say no when they mean yes, and drive a man out of his wits just for the fun of it."

_____

_____

_____

_____

_____

_____

_____

_____

_____

_____

_____

_____

_____

_____

_____

_____

_____

_____

_____

_____

_____

"I don't like to doze by the fire. I like adventures, and I'm going to find some."

"Thank goodness, I can always find something funny to keep me up."

"She is too fond of books, and it has turned her brain."

"If you feel your value lies in being merely decorative, I fear that someday you might find yourself believing that's all that you really are."

"For the sincere wish to be good is half the battle."

"There, I've done my best. If that wont do, I shall have to wait till I can do better."

_____

_____

_____

_____

_____

_____

_____

_____

_____

_____

_____

_____

_____

_____

_____

_____

_____

_____

_____

_____

_____

_____

"The girls put their wits to work, and - necessity being the mother of invention - made whatever they needed."

"You have a good many little gifts and virtues, but there is no need of parading them, for conceit spoils the finest genius."

"But the spirit of Eve is strong in all her daughters."

"Have regular hours for work and play, make each day both useful and pleasant, and prove that you understand the worth of time by employing it well."

"It takes so little to make a child happy, that it is a pity in a world full of sunshine and pleasant things, that there should be any wistful faces, empty hands, or lonely little hearts."

"Nothing is impossible to a determined woman."

"Even a fair table may become a pulpit, if it can offer the good and helpful words which are never out of season."

"A faithful friend is a strong defense, and he that hath found him hath found a treasure."

"I rather miss my wild girl, but if I get a strong, helpful, tender-hearted woman in her place, I shall feel quite satisfied."

"Oh dear, life is pretty tough sometimes, isn't it?"

"Life is like college, may I graduate and earn some honors."

"Fame is a pearl many dive for and only a few bring up. Even when they do, it is not perfect, and they sigh for more, and lose better things in struggling for them."

"I think she is growing up, and so begins to dream dreams, and have hopes and fears and fidgets, without knowing why or being able to explain them."

"Be worthy love, and love will come."

She is unlike any girl I ever saw, there's no sentimentality about her, she is wise, and kind, and sweet. She says what she means, looks you straight in the eye, and is as true as steel."

"Education is not confined to books, and the finest characters often graduate from no college, but make experience their master, and life their book."

"Kindness in looks and words and ways is true politeness, and any one can have it if they only try to treat other people as they like to be treated themselves."

"Women work a good many miracles..."

"Watch and pray, dear, never get tired of trying, and never think it is impossible to conquer your fault."

"A happy soul in a healthy body makes the best sort of beauty for man or woman."

"...but I know, by experience, how much genuine happiness can be had in a plain little house, where the daily bread is earned, and some privations give sweetness to the few pleasures."

"That is a good book it seems to me, which is opened with expectation and closed with profit."

"I'd rather take coffee than compliments just now."

"Gentlemen, be courteous to the old maids, no matter how poor and plain and prim, for the only chivalry worth having is that which is the readiest to to pay deference to the old, protect the feeble..."

"I've got the key to my castle in the air, but whether I can unlock the door remains to be seen."

"I don't want a fashionable wedding, but only those about me whom I love, and to them I wish to look and be my familiar self."

"Men are always ready to die for us, but not to make our lives worth having. Cheap sentiment and bad logic."

"I keep turning over new leaves, and spoiling them, as I used to spoil my copybooks, and I make so many beginnings there never will be an end."

"He was the first, the only love her life, and in a nature like hers such passions take deep root and die-hard."

"Strong convictions precede great actions."

"I am not afraid of storms, for I am learning how to sail my ship."

"The power of finding beauty in the humblest things makes home happy and life lovely."

"Some books are so familiar that reading them is like being home again."

"Good, old-fashioned ways keep hearts sweet, heads sane, hands busy."

_____

_____

_____

_____

_____

_____

_____

_____

_____

_____

_____

_____

_____

_____

_____

_____

_____

_____

_____

_____

_____

_____

_____

"Love should not make us blind to faults, nor familiarity make us too ready to blame the shortcomings we see."

"Young men often laugh at the sensible girls whom they secretly respect, and affect to admire the silly ones whom they secretly despise."

"We don't choose our talents, but we needn't hide them in a napkin because they are not just what we want."

"My dear, don't let the sun go down upon your anger - forgive each other, help each other and begin again tomorrow."

"We all have our temptations, some far greater than yours, and it often takes us all our lives to conquer them."

"Love is a great beautifier."

"Many argue, not many converse."

"But young as she was, Jo had learned that hearts, like flowers, cannot be rudely handled, but must open naturally"

"Dear me! how happy and good we'd be, if we had no worries!"

"I want to do something splendid...something heroic or wonderful that won't be forgotten after I'm dead. I don't know what, but I'm on the watch for it and mean to astonish you all someday."

"Prosperity suits some people, and they blossom best in a glow of sunshine, others need the shade, and are the sweeter for a touch of frost."

"take up your little burdens again, for though they seem heavy sometimes, they are good for us, and lighten as we learn to carry them."

"She fell into the moody, miserable state of mind which often comes when strong wills have to yield to the inevitable."

"It is an excellent plan to have some place where we can go to be quiet, when things vex or grieve us."

"There can't be too much charity!"

"I shall keep my book on the table here, and read a little every morning as soon as I wake, for I know it will do me good, and help me through the day."

"She preferred imaginary heroes to real ones, because when tired of them, the former could be shut up in the tin kitchen till called for, and the latter were less manageable."

Made in United States
Troutdale, OR
12/06/2024